D1542043

FAMOUS TEXAS ★ OUTHOUSES

AND OTHER B.S.

D.N. "BIG DON" PAGE

Library of Congress Cataloging-in-Publication data
ISBN 0-9679609-0-8
1. Humor - Fiction.
Printed In China

Table of Contents

FOREWORD AND BACKWARD
(The Passing of the Texas Outhouse)

The legendary Texas outhouse has always played an important role in history of the Lone Star State. Great Texas names like Sam Houston, The Lone Star State's first President and Judge Roy Bean and his "Law west of the Pecos," both used outhouses. Davy Crocket will always be remembered for his stand at the Alamo. Let's not forget Pancho Villa. He spent more time in Texas than he did in Mexico! Fellow Texans, let's make no mistake about it. No matter how famous a person is or was, there is always one thing that we all share in common. That's the morning "constitutional!" People, let me tell you when we all gotta go, we gotta go!

As we progress through these hallowed pages, you will get a firsthand look at the monuments some of these folks left behind in memory of their own "behinds." You will see how they architecturally influenced their personal private chamber of "blissful relief." One request, please: if you are a house guest and reading this Texas novel while on the "John," don't forget yourself and think these pages are like those of a Sears catalog and tear them out to wipe! Thank you.

"THE OUTLAW QUEEN'S "THRONE"

BELLE STARR: NOTORIOUS TEXAS BANDIT QUEEN

What a gal! Rougher than a cob! Tougher than a Texas boot-heel! Sweeter than honey! And soft as pussy-cat fur! She was all that and more! Myra Maybelle Shirley was a well-educated young lady from an upper middle-class family that was attracted to outlaw trash like Cole Younger, Jim Reed and Sam Starr.

As tough a lady as Belle was, she had a phobia that was never revealed until after her tragic death in 1889. Belle Starr, the fearless woman of the plains, was afraid of the dark! Her daughter, Pearl Younger, made that public information after her mom was blown off her horse by a shotgun blast! The unknown assailant was never caught.

A few years back, Belle had a nice big home with an outhouse, it was said, she designed herself. It had two nice tall columns in front with a facade containing a big star. On the roof-peak above the star she had a bell mounted. Asked by a neighbor, "why," Belle replied "Well, read it, who does it say lives here?" The neighbor was impressed!

Belle built that two-holer outhouse for the purpose of hiding her secret. It was a well-known fact that Belle would never venture out for a nighttime pee unless she had a place for her company to sit close by.

Come to think of it, if I was sitting next to this notorious woman of the old west in a pitch black two-holer outhouse, I'd be afraid of the dark too!

QUESTION:
Where did the Texas expression "rougher than a cob" come from?

ANSWER:
Back when material to "wipe" with was hard to come by, after a relieving visit to the outhouse, an enterprising ranch-hand stumbled onto a great discovery! After "shucking" a wagon load of corn for the livestock, unknowingly a few of the corn-cobs found their way into his levi's pants pockets.

A hurried trip to the outhouse found him without newspaper or catalog to clean himself up with. Noticing the "cobs" in his pockets, he decided to try them as a substitute for paper and it worked! It was painful, but it worked! The idea of using corn-cobs spread quickly and they soon became standard in all outhouses as a back-up for paper.

If you have ever rubbed your hand over a corn-cob and related it to a very tender body part, you will quickly know where this old Texas expression came from!

ODE TO THE SEARS CATALOG

Oh! you wonderful Sears catalog,
with your pages so soft and bright,
They are the ones we tear out first, so
we can gently wipe!

Your slick and shiny pages
are always the last to use...
They must be ``crinkled'' up really good,
so our ass we won't abuse.

Oh! you wonderful Sears catalog,
in the outhouse you are lord,
everyone prefers you two to one
over good old Monkey Ward!

Irene Woolworth

SAM'S PLACE

PRESIDENT OF TEXAS: SAM HOUSTON

Little "Sammie" Houston was a good kid. He was smart, curious and a fair student. His mother didn't care too much for him hanging around with that Indian chief, Jolly, though. The chief taught Sam how to smoke and hunt and fish like a good Cherokee, which was all to his benefit in later years. Sam also loved the river and the paddle wheel steamers that ruled the water. Sam wanted to be a riverboat pilot, but as history would have it, he grew up to become a General, a Governor, a Congressman, Senator and finally, the President of the Texas Republic.

Sam was especially noted for his defeat of the Mexican General, Santa Anna, in 1836 at San Jacinto. When President Houston decided to spend his last years in Huntsville, Texas, he had a home built that had all the resemblances of a riverboat. It looked just like a land-locked steamer. If that sounds a little funny to you, take a trip to Huntsville and see for yourself!

Now, about the outhouse. The architect who designed the Houston home was going to surprise Sam with an original outhouse design that would "knock his boots off!" Unfortunately, Sam died before ever seeing the outhouse on the adjoining page.

Do you think he would have liked it?

MADE IN "FLUSHING, NEW YAWK"

GENEVIEVE JACKSON GOES TO "NEW YAWK CITY"

Texas ranch wives are no different than any other kind of wife when it comes to the "I wants." I want this, or I want that, is a common cry heard by all husbands worldwide. Genevieve Jackson, old man Jackson's young, second wife, was one of the best "I wanters" in the entire Lone Star State. God, could she want!

She wanted to go to "New Yawk" City real bad! She got her way and off they went to "New Yawk." "Times Square, here we come!" No sooner they got there, the "I wants" started. " Gen," as she was called for short, was so fascinated by the new fangled overhead flush-boxes in Gimbels' ladies room, she had to have one. Mind you, there were no flush toilets at the ranch, just a regular old outhouse. Gen loved to pull the chain and hear the water "gush" down. She did it 10 times a day. Back home at the ranch with Gen's new toy foolishly installed for no useful purpose, visitors came by the wagon load to view the "flusher." This was too much for old man Jackson and he presented frivolous Genevieve with an "I want" of his own, which was quickly granted...a divorce!

PANCHO'S OUTHOUSE VILLA!

PANCHO VILLA AND HIS SOMBRERO

Can you imagine an outhouse being built for a person just to accommodate his hat? That's what they did for good ole' pancho!

Pancho Villa, as every Texan knows, was revered by the Mexicans and cussed by the U.S. Federal Government. The "Feds" even had General "Black Jack" Pershing down in Texas chasing that evil "bandito."

Pancho always wore his sombrero. He had many and they were all made with the biggest, widest, brims ever! He was never seen without his head covered. Some say he was bald, others say that a federalista bullet creased his "cabeza" (head). Trips to the old one-holer outhouse were always a wild scene. He would fuss and fume trying to get his hat in with him and it would always wind up outside in the dirt.

Finally, Miguel Sanchez, Pancho's handyman, seeing his boss so distressed at least 7 or 8 times a day, built him the custom outhouse you see pictured. Talk about "peace" overtaking such a notorious outlaw during his moment of private labor, Miguel's outhouse made him a very peaceful soul.

My "Stetson" is off to Miguel.

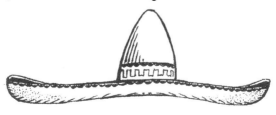

SOOPER-DOOPER-PORTABLE-POOPER!

PORTER'S PORTABLE POTTY

Coleman Porter was always looking for a new way to make money. He was not the most ambitious Texan that ever graced the Lone Star State, but he was surely one of the most enterprising. He was one of the first to haul a stock tank to a county fair, fill it with fish he seined from the river and charged 3 cents to use a pole he made. Hook and bait were included. You could keep what you caught. Mr. Porter was also the genius that rigged up a cotton bale weigher to guess the fairgoer's weight. He contrived it to weigh within 3 pounds of what he guessed and hardly ever lost. This was a real money maker until the sheriff figured out he was cheating the customers and closed him down.

Noticing that most everyone, himself included, had to head behind a building or woods to relieve themselves. Cole hit upon another brilliant idea: A portable outhouse! He found a one-holer, rigged a washtub under the hole and mounted it on cotton-wagon wheels. It was quite a dazzling sight when he would go to family reunions, civic gatherings, chiverees and even a hanging once. He called it "Porter's Portable Potty," or "PP," for short. The "PP" was a very successful enterprise and when the more brazen cowpokes would ask him how much money he could make with that contraption, he would always answer, "A shit-pot full!"

THE WIDE OPEN SPACES OF TEXAS

THE "CHEAP BASTARD"

This world is full of "weird" people and I guess Texas has its share of them. I hate to admit that any Texan would be nothing other than a fine, upstanding, God-fearing, go-to-church-on Sunday, neighborly kind of a human being! Amen to that brother! Then, there is this wealthy cheap bastard that has as much acreage, or more, than the King boys in south Texas. I hate to call him his given name so I call him C.B. (and you know what that stands for.) It should be C.B.S.O.B. Now that's even better! There have been many a tales been told about C.B. and I know they are true. The one that stands out in my mind is the time I visited his place in the valley. C.B. wasn't home, thank the Lord, and if I had not seen with my own two eyes what I saw, I would have called the teller a bald faced liar. But, there it was: An outhouse with only two sides! It was sitting about 200 yards away from C.B.'s very nice English tudor type home. On closer inspection, and I might add "utility," too, I realized what C.B. did. He built two sides, put them together like a "V", built a floor, a seat and a funny tin roof. He faced it away from the house so no one could see the occupier. Also, from the house, if you did not see the Texas flag flying, it was busy and you could save yourself a long trip down the path. I asked the ranch foreman why such a crazy way to build an outhouse. His answer was quick! "The cheap bastard didn't have to pay extra for two sides and a door."

GRIMM'S "WHIM"

THE TOWN UNDERTAKER

I.M. Grimm, a perfect name for an undertaker if I ever heard one, was just exactly that. His first name was Isadore. Isadore Mortimer Grimm was his full name. "Izzy," his townspeople nickname, was not what you would call a "fun" person to be around. In fact, he was kinda "Grim." His reputation as a funeral director was the best. Mr. Grimm's funerals were always solemn, dignified and inexpensive. "Izzy" did have a passion that was his secret. He loved, absolutely adored, the shape of a casket! In fact, when it came time to build an additional outhouse on the funeral grounds, Mr. Grimm took over! The picture you see on the opposite page is what he came up with and had built—grave flowerpots and all. One time when business was brisk and storage was limited, Mr. Grimm had to put the ancient, newly deceased P.T. Turnberry's corpse in the outhouse for safekeeping. As luck would have it, damned if P.T.'s old lady happened by and decided she needed to "go." The double funeral for Mr. and Mrs. P.T. Turnberry was held at 2:00 p.m. the following Sunday.

THIS IS NOT YOUR TYPICAL TEXAS "LEAN-TO"

THE LEANING OUTHOUSE ON "LOVER'S LANE"

Italy may have it's leaning "Tower of Pisa," but Dallas has it's own "Leaning Outhouse." Perhaps not as many tourists come from all over the world to visit the "leaner" on Lovers Lane. But it sure attracts a lot of local Texans. The same mystery that boggled the minds of scientists about the tower in Italy confounds the same minds in Texas about the outhouse on Lovers Lane. When you put the corner posts down 5 feet to bed-rock and build up from there, hey, that should be one solid crapper! Wouldn't you agree? Apparently, not so. Mr. Wilder Bunch, (his real name, honest) and Dr. L.C. Smith, both from the civil engineering department at nearby SMU (Southern Methodist University), dropped by at the owner's request to have a "look-see." After much "hmmmmm'ing" and a lot of "ahhhh'ing," they both concluded that it was the result of an earthquake. There has never been an earthquake in the history of Dallas before, so why now? Dr. Smith said it was a slight tremor right through the center of the outhouse and dropped one side 8 inches. A phenomenon, indeed! The owner let it stay that way as it was still usable. They did have to put up a "hold bar" on the down-side. That was after Jose, the gardener who had "the runs" wasn't quick enough. He messed all over the seat, slid down hard in his own mess, hit the wall and broke his collar bone!

'Betcha the leaning tower in Pisa never had that kind of excitement!

"TEX" TOLLIVER DIED IN 1883
WENT FROM ONE "HOLE" TO ANOTHER

THE OUTHOUSE TOMBSTONE

In Bexar County, Texas, there is a grave with a headstone in the shape of an outhouse. Unusual as gravestones go. It sure attracts a lot of attention for the person buried beneath it. That person was Elijah "Tex" Tolliver. "Tex" was a native of Bexar, County and in his entire lifetime never wandered across the county line. His trade was building outhouses and it kept him too busy to do any fancy traveling or even take a wife. He was the best and the Bexar County folk loved him for his dedicated art.

You can look on his tombstone and see the year he died, 1883. You also can see by the tombstone that the Bexar County people did something special for Elijah Tolliver by the custom built headstone. One thing that the folk don't mention is the way he died. So happens he was replacing an outhouse seat at one of the areas "Bawdy Houses." Remember, "Tex" was now 69 years old and a little bit unsteady. Well, he lost his balance, fell head-first into the soft mess below and was asphyxiated.

All I could ever get any one to comment on his passing was best said by George Pope, the barber. He said, "It was a shitty way to go!"

"WHERE'S MAMA?"

DAVY CROCKET:
"KING OF THE WILD RACCOON HATS"

All Texans know that Davy Crocket wasn't born and reared here in Texas, but as Texans we also know that he got here as fast as he could! When he did come, what in the devil was he wearing on his head but a stinky, moth-eaten raccoon hat! "Real" Texans tried all out to get him to wear Stetson! A cowboy hat was what he needed to wear in the Lone Star State. But no, it wouldn't look proper with the rest of his "woodsy" attire. Even General Sam Houston tried to convince that he might get shot at for being mistaken for a "woods pussy" or something! Davy took a lot of joking about his furry headpiece.

The most memorable incident was when he was boarding at the old Rainey place. A few of the boys got together, shot a few 'coons and somehow "wove" their tails together to make one huge raccoon tail. Then, they jammed it in under the roof in the back of the outhouse. When they called Davy's attention to it, he yelled something about it must be the biggest 'coon in Texas! He ran in the house to get his rifle. When he came a runnin' out ready to blast that 'coon, the boys yelled "Whoa, Davy!" They didn't want him shoot'n old man Rainey's outhouse to pieces! They all had a good laugh about it. Even Davy smiled a little. Any further effort to change Davy over to a cowboy hat always fell on deaf ears and Davy continued to wear that mess on his head until he met his fate at the Alamo. We often wonder if they buried it with him?

THE OUTHOUSE NAMED
"LILY BOUQUET"

THE "HONORABLE" JUDGE ROY BEAN

"The law west of the Pecos" was the claim the Judge revered the most. As a saloonkeeper and a justice of the peace, he was a real S.O.B.! This Texan was not too well liked by the many gamblers, rustlers and thieves that lived in his town of Langtry, Texas. He named the town after Lily Langtry, the English actress he was madly in love with. Even the saloon he owned was called "the Jersey Lily" in her honor. The Judge became very fearful of his many enemies in the town. He couldn't hire any bodyguards for fear of being gunned down by the guys he hired to protect him. His outhouse was his refuge. He called it his "Lily Bouquet," again in her honor. Word had it that it sure didn't smell like a bunch of flowers after the Judge had been in there awhile! Since the armor plate and peek-slits were on all four sides, Roy Bean, felt quite secure in the "Lily Bouquet."

The Judge died a natural death in 1904 and the old-timers always said it was the protective iron-plate of "Lily Bouquet" that kept him from being "dry-gulched" and killed!

After the Judge died, Caleb Garrett, the town deputy, just to see what would happen, took out his 45 and put a shot right where the judge would be reposing. Dam'nd if'n that bullet went clean through one side and out the other!

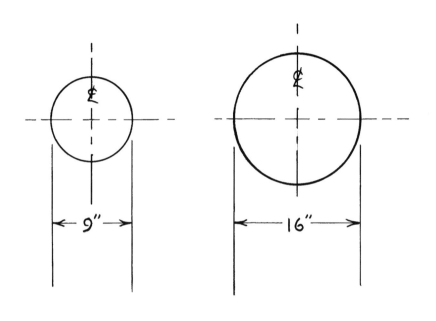

LEGAL   ILLEGAL

City of Bowie, TX.
Ord. # 1537583894 D-6

THE OUTHOUSE HOLE-SIZE ORDINANCE OF BOWIE, TEXAS

In 1881, the city council of Bowie, Texas put a bid out for a two-hole outhouse to be built at the local fairgrounds. Heretofore, there had been no place for the local townspeople to relieve themselves in a sanitary manner.

Rufus Titus, a carpenter of sorts, won the contract for $32.50. Twenty-eight days later, the new facility was ready for use. Rufus did a right nice job and was given a $5 bonus by the mayor.

After the very first civic function at the fairgrounds and the god-awful language directed at the mayor and his council by three furiously irate mothers, the mayor probably wished he had his $5 back!

What had happened to cause such a fuss goes back to our craftsman, Rufus Titus. Rufus, hardly being a Harvard educated outhouse architect did the best he knew with limited abilities. Not knowing what size to cut the holes in the seat, he made them a generous 16 inches in diameter. Now that is a pretty good sized hole by any standards. After the third little four-year-old lost his balance and fell, squish, into the ugly mess below, something had to be done. Not only were the mothers upset, but so was the entire volunteer fire department that had to rescue these little tykes, scrub them clean while they screamed bloody murder and return them to their furious moms!

The very next council meeting produced an ordinance that prohibited (and backed up by a $100 fine), any outhouse built within the Bowie City limits from having a hole in the seat no larger than nine inches in diameter!

Mr. Titus had to re-do the hole sizes at the fairgrounds, plus pay for it out of his own pocket. There went his $5 bonus! Down the hole with the rest of the mess!

To this day, there has never been another case of the volunteer fire department rescuing another child from an outhouse by falling through the hole-in-one!

MY UNCLE RUDY AND HIS
CHAMBER POT

My uncle Rudy was a meticulous, thirtyish, bachelor fellow that lived at home with his mother. He slept upstairs on the second floor in a large room with two double beds separated by a big dresser. Unfortunately for him, like so many homes built in the 1890s, there was no bathroom with a potty on the second floor. Uncle Rudy solved that problem, as was the norm back then, with a white porcelain, flower decorated, chamber pot.

When I was a little kid, I would visit my grandma, who was also my uncle Rudy's mom, and would sleep in the upstairs double bed across from uncle Rudy. About four a.m. in the morning, the crystal-clear tinkling sound of water hitting water in a dead-quiet dark room can sound like a wild Texas rainstorm with thunder loud enough to shake you out of bed! It was frightening to a little boy, but I never uttered a sound and would soon fall back to sleep.

I never dared to ask my uncle and it has been a mystery to me all these years, how, in the dark of night, standing up, how he could hit that nine inch hole and never miss! In the morning, down he would come with the chamber pot, empty it, rinse it, fill it with clean water and set it back at the foot of the stairs ready to take up for another nights use. Chamber pots are antique items now and on occasion when I spot one in an antique shop I have to overcome the challenge to buy one, take it home and see if I could hit that nine-inch hole, standing up in the dark like my uncle Rudy!

"SADDLE-ASS HENRY": THE TEXAS "BUFFALO" HORSE SOLDIER

There never was known a rougher, tougher, meaner-than-a-rattlesnake buffalo soldier than Henry "Saddle-ass" Bible. Born and reared in the Panhandle, Henry was dirty, smelled of liquor and would bite your ear plumb off if you ever had to fight him! How he ever made it through troop inspections is a big mystery. Most think he was just "passed" over because headquarters tried to discipline Henry a thousand times before and failed.

Now, drinking on post was an absolute No! No!, but not for Trooper Bible. Henry had bottles of "John Barleycorn" stashed all over the compound and as a result, Henry was 'tipsy, most of the time. Even if a hundred miles away from any saloon, 'Ole Henry had his daily snort of booze.

Outhouses in the army were called "latrines." It was always smart to remember to pitch your pup-tent upwind of the latrine so the smell wouldn't kill you! To build an army regulation latrine on patrol was an art. Everything in the army has to be the exact measurement. A standard field latrine is a rectangle shape eight-feet long, four-feet wide and five-feet deep. That's a pretty good-sized hole in the ground.

Next, we have to build a "seat." To do this chore, you chop down two, four-inch minimum diameter, sapling trees with a crotch. The crotch should be able to hold a tree limb of the same diameter. Now you plant a crotched tree-trunk on each side of the hole and lay the straight tree-trunk across it and "eureka" a seat! Before using, always remember to grab a handful of paper or leaves before you drop your pants and carefully sit down!

Back to Trooper Henry. Once, while on bivouac, he was drunker than 'Cooter Brown when he got out of bed in the black of night and staggered down to the latrine. While sitting on the tree limb and reaching for some leaves to "wipe" Henry lost his balance and straight down he goes. Good thing he passed out on the way down.

At "reveille" the first thing the troopers do is run down to the latrine to do their "business." That's when 'ole Saddle-Ass woke up in the bottom of the pit in all that mess and let out a yell that scared the hell out of all the troopers "crapping" all over Henry Bible!

It took the better part of a day and a lot of saddle soap and disinfectant to clean stinky Henry up. Henry lived to be 88 years old and is buried near Ft. Davis, Texas.

It is rumored that Henry served out his enlistment, was honorably discharged with a pension and after that latrine "fiasco" never took another drink of "John Barleycorn" for the rest of his natural life!

Sgt. Amos T. Pricer, 6th U.S. Cav. (Ret.)

"HAVE A SEAT"

THE FLOWERY PATH TO THE OUTHOUSE

Every time some silly,cow-herder cowboy rancher puts up an outhouse, he sticks it so far back on the spread that you need an eagle's eye to see it, let alone get to it! Getting to it! Now that's another problem. Probably the biggest reason you can't find one when you need one is that they hid them so dang'ed good. When you need one more times than not, you need one in a big hurry!

Getting to the "privy," as some city dudes call it, should not be a long and dangerous trip. The "laws" 'ought to step in and demand that all outhouses be no more than 50 steps from the back door. It sure would save a lot of underwear from getting dirty 'cause the trip was too dad-burned long!

Big rocks, barbed-wire, tin-cans and broken bottles should be outlawed from the path to the outhouse. I can show you scars on my 'dawgs that prove why barefooted trip in the dark could cause such a bloody mess!

My daddy, the Lord rest his soul, always had a lantern and matches ready for a nighttime trip. He always made a nice, smooth path to the "Little House" and mother always planted flowers on either side.

I always admired daddy for being such a well-organized planner of outhouses. I never had the heart to tell him that even with his easy and safe-to-use facility in the dark, I would just step outside the door and pee on mother's flowers.

And mother in her sweet and curious way, could never figure out why her flowers near the back door were so much bigger and bushier than the rest along the path the outhouse.

P.S. I never had the heart to tell her why either.

Senator W.M.S. "Bubba" Goldsmith

THE OUTHOUSE SPIDER

I'm a spider in waiting, I wait a bunch!
That's what I do, if I expect to eat lunch.

I was born in this outhouse,
been here quite a spell.

A great place to live,
except for the smell.

The flies come here often,
"Free food!" is their cry,

Little do they know
they're about to die!

I spin my web and
the flies get caught.

I do my job well,
just like I was taught.

But I am a spider and
I like to bite!

All outhouse users
are my special "delight."

I like to wait,
just under the hole.

Right near the edge
that's always my goal.

I'm an outhouse spider
and I enjoy a good laugh!

And when someone sits down,
to make the "necessary" pass.

Up I jump and
bite their ass!

Author unknown
(and wants to stay that way)

BILLY JOE BOB OF PLAINVIEW, TEXAS SEZ...
THE END